Midwest Anecdotes, Superstitions and Remedies

By

SANDRA L. DUDLEY

A division of Squire Publishers, Inc.
4500 College Blvd.
Leawood, KS 66211
1/888/888-7696

Copyright 2001
Printed in the United States

ISBN: 1-58597-108-1

Library of Congress Control Number:
2001096817

A division of Squire Publishers, Inc.
4500 College Blvd.
Leawood, KS 66211
1/888/888-7696

Dedication

This book is dedicated to all of those who suffered through my English I and English II classes from 1985 to 2000 at Fort Scott Community College. If there be errors of identification, please allow for my haste in both grading and returning the paper before the semester ended and before final exams while at the same time collecting this wealth of relevant information. Then, too, teaching the pronoun use was, many times, an exercise in futility, and by the time any confusion could be corrected, the students had long since left for other colleges or for future jobs. Also, what is recorded is taken out of context from the seven to ten or fifteen-page papers. I hope clarity is merely not assumed but understood. Thank you, students.

A special thanks also to President Richard Hedges and Dr. Laura Meeks, Dean of Instruction, administrators at Fort Scott Community College in 1985 who gave me free rein and bent to pursue the innovations which I believed would be both beneficial and necessary for quality writing in our college. Each administrator had the humble good grace to allow for eccentricity and uniqueness if those qualities ensured a commitment to the objectives of our English Department. To have this vote of confidence was an instrumental, positive influence in my teaching career at Fort Scott Community College from 1985 to 2000. Thank you.

Editor's Note

In 1985, at Fort Scott Community College, I became disillusioned with the traditional research paper and the increased tendency of the student to "copy" or "paraphrase" information without regard to proper credit or documentation. This habit is cultivated very early in grade schools when reports are assigned from encyclopedias and renforced in higher grades with the necessity of "bonus points" and make-up work in order to sustain eligibility education. The addition of the internet has, of course, exacerbated the problems in accountability.

Therefore, in 1985, I designed what I thought to be a unique method of research whereby my English students would research three generations on one side of their family, either the mother or father's side, beginning with a great-grandparent and ending with their immediate family. That report would include both facts and human interests such as patterns, firsts, anecdotes, sayings, remedies, superstitions, and happy and unhappy events.

What resulted was a cornucopia of original, interesting stories and myths which quickly evolved into patterns representing a culture endemic to our area of Kansas, Missouri, Oklahoma, and Nebraska. While research went beyond these borders, basically the history involved the same locales, and by 1988 I realized what a gold mine I had and what a joy it was to accumulate these treasures. Many times I would come home from teaching to read these stories to my mother, and by so doing, I soon came to recognize that perhaps others would likewise enjoy the humor of such stories that reflect our rural Midwest culture.

Anecdotes

Matt Altieri's grandfather was left-handed, but the nuns would beat the knuckles on his left hand to make him write right-handed. This same relative ate so much ice cream, his stomach froze *(Matt Altieri)*.

* * * * *

Her great-great-grandpa, Wilhelm, helped name the city of Jerusalem, North Dakota. In a town meeting, no one could agree what to call the town. Wilhelm got aggravated, and when leaving said, "I don't give a damn if you call it Jerusalem. I am going home." So they named the town Jerusalem *(Jennifer Wallace)*.

* * * * *

His great-grandfather was born in a two-room sod house in Frontier County, Nebraska, in 1891. Since he weighed but two pounds, his aunt could put her wedding ring over his arm *(Hal Messersmith)*.

* * * * *

His great-great-grandfather had a relative who had a woodpile in his yard. However, people kept walking by and helping themselves to his wood, so he hollowed out a piece of wood and filled it with gun powder. Soon, smoke was coming out of a neighbor's house *(Garret Zohner)*.

* * * * *

Grandpa's brothers loved making their sisters' lives miserable. They were cleaning out the outhouse and hauling it away in big barrels on a wagon. Les hit a bump on purpose, and his sister, Ellen, fell in the barrel head first *(Lori George)*.

* * * * *

Another time, these same brothers needed a banjo for their band, so they killed the sister's pet cat and used the skin for the banjo *(Lori George)*.

* * * * *

My grandpa would give me candy (usually orange slices) and sing a song about a little girl who got her nose stuck in the butter! Now I cannot find anyone who remembers the words to that song *(Bill Egidy)*.

* * * * *

My granddad ("Pap") could wiggle his ears. I was the only grandchild who learned how to do it. When I did, Pap would say, "I really eat that shit up." When Pap died, they gave him a twenty-one gun salute, and I thought to myself, "Pap would really eat this shit up." My brother and I and four of our cousins were pallbearers. That was one of the saddest days of my whole life. Pap had a bronze star and a Purple Heart from battles in World War II in Belgium *(Troy Flaharty)*.

* * * * *

People didn't send their kids to high school around Hepler, Kansas, because they thought it would raise their taxes *(Nathan Woodward)*.

* * * * *

I was eleven years old at the time, and my granddad thought the bull acted like it was going to chase me. Granddad picked up a rock, threw it at the bull, and hit it in the head. The bull fell over dead as a doornail. He became known as "Bull Durham" *(Shannon Ledbetter)*.

* * * * *

The relatives always called my mother "the cutest little tumor I ever saw" because when the grandmother was in labor, an aunt told her it might just be a tumor *(Sarah Shook)*.

* * * * *

A Northern soldier burned his great-great-great-grandfather's grist mill at Pappinsville, Missouri, which was the first grist mill this side of Mississippi. When the

Northern soldiers burned the mill, they transported the smoke stacks to Lenith, Kansas, to build a bridge which still stands today. Lenith also contains the first Masonic Lodge in Kansas *(Danny Reagan)*.

* * * * *

My grandmother (age seven) walked into a four-foot snowdrift and got stuck. Her brother ran off and left. After an hour and a half, a neighbor found her and took her home. It took four to five hours to thaw out her legs. Years later, neighbors dropped in to inquire about the small daughter who froze *(Vicki Chadd)*.

* * * * *

Her mother's mother was run over by a wagon wheel at age five. The wheel went right over her back. When they picked her up, her mouth was bleeding, so they loaded her into the wagon. After a short journey, the horse's bridle bit broke and the wagon ran into a ditch bank, throwing the mother and grandmother out. They took the grandmother to a doctor. He had her jump onto a table, jump off and run around the table. After this exercise, she was perfectly all right *(Brenda Bailey)*.

* * * * *

When her grandmother got married, her father was so poor that he sold a hog for $8 to buy her a rolling pin, wash tub and a washboard for a wedding present *(Robbin Wessels)*.

* * * * *

A great-grandmother was born to a black woman and a Navajo Indian. The plantation hands started to hang the Indian, and the owner saved his life *(Lisa Hatter)*.

* * * * *

Her grandfather spoke only broken English. The family tells how he never owned a car, but he drove his tractor to town in Arma, Kansas, whenever he needed supplies, groceries or a haircut. Once he was hit from behind, and when the policeman arrived on the scene, he asked the tractor driver if he had used a hand signal. The grandfather replied, "If the S.O.B. didn't see my tractor, how would he see my hand signal?" *(Wendi Anselmi)*.

* * * * *

Granddad Shrader ran off the road at Meadowlark Lane. Ten years later, his father ran off the road in the exact same spot. "We believe there might be a boogie man living down that road." Also Bryan's grandmother was born two months premature and weighed but four pounds. She was fed with an eyedropper and kept in a bed made from a metal soup-cracker tin. Heated bricks in blankets were used for the incubator *(Bryan Shrader)*.

* * * * *

His grandma asked him what he wanted for breakfast. He said, "An egg without the white." She fixed it that way, and he wrote, "It made me feel so important" *(Kendall Ewing).*

* * * * *

Garland, Kansas, used to be called Memphis, Kansas. Those were wicked, wicked times back then *(Tim Clary).*

* * * * *

A relative was run off of the farm for not saying the rosary and was not heard from again. Another relative (ten years old) was found shot in a cornfield *(Mona Farrell).*

* * * * *

Her great-grandmother saw a ball of fire three times in life. Each time, a tragedy happened in their lives *(Julie Elder).*

* * * * *

Grandma's dog bit the mailman on the thigh. Grandma had the mailman drop his pants right outside while she inspected the bite! *(Brent Chance).*

* * * * *

A relative found ten dollars and bought a month's supply of groceries *(Amber Russell).*

* * * * *

He is the relative of a descendant of Lord

Baltimore Calvert, founder of Baltimore, Maryland *(Dale Goode)*.

* * * * *

Her aunt was blind and raised seven children. Also, a grandmother turned grey at age eighteen *(Teresa Davis)*.

* * * * *

A relative's father invented the oxcart, but the Germans stole it. In time, people discovered the truth *(Rosemary Alpizar)*.

* * * * *

A relative's ears were cut off by bushwhackers during the Civil War *(Brian Smith)*.

* * * * * * * * *

We had a relative who smoked a pipe when she drove her horse and buggy. She kept the tobacco in a bag and lemon drops in the same bag. Periodically, she gave the lemon drops to grandchildren, but the drops smelled so of tobacco that they gave them to the horse. It got so the horse expected the lemon drops *(Marcia Hart)*.

* * * * *

On June 23, 1923, a relative was married and then kidnapped by friends and taken to a cabin where she was kept from the groom for twenty-four hours *(Jenny Carroll)*.

* * * * *

People asked his dad why they had so

many kids (six), and his dad replied, "It was the only way to get the rocks picked up out of the fields (Jim Bob Weil).

* * * * *

Her great-great-grandmother, Bessie Mae Lee, was a fourth cousin to Robert E. Lee. She died, and since the body was not found for several days, her dog ate her remains (Hannah Kenyon).

* * * * *

Her grandma said that one day she got fed up with a neighbor beating his wife. She and another lady tied him to a pole and horsewhipped him. He never beat his wife again (Toni Cummings).

* * * * *

An uncle said, "In 1663, the Websters would hang witches. Today, we pay them alimony" (Matt Webster).

* * * * *

The brothers in the father's family used to give the chickens enemas (Laura Wunderly).

* * * * *

A baby was thought to be dead coming over on the boat from Red River, Austria, to the United States. They started to bury him at sea when he began to cry (Vance Katze).

* * * * *

His grandfather's standard reply to having to do chores was, "Yea, sure, and I could stick a broom up my ass and sweep the floor, too" (Brad Nelson).

* * * * *

About his great-grandpa: He spent plenty of time with grandchildren teaching them to sing and to dance on a summer day and to lie on our backs and imagine what shapes the clouds were. He took kids to county fairs, to the horse races, and fed us our favorite gum — but we had to find it first (Phil Trivette).

* * * * *

A boy's grandfather had his hands smashed in a steel company accident. What was left of his finger was sewn into two short finger stubs. The boy once asked his grandpa how he lost his fingers? "Well, I was picking my nose like you and your cousin were just doing, and the boogers ate my fingers off." The boy said that he never picked his nose again. Incidentally, the Grandpa was given $17.81 in compensation for the accident (Seth Needham).

* * * * *

She says that her dad would not tolerate a lazy man. One time she remembers picking up pears and then working in the garden. She told her dad that she was getting tired and asked if he wasn't tired also. He replied, "I don't know. How does it feel to be tired?" (Carla Slaughter).

* * * * *

A grandfather was shot in a barroom brawl (Scott Drennan).

* * * * *

His great-grandfather lit firecrackers under his parents' bed. "Boy, I got my hide tanned for that one," said the great-grandfather (Kevin Ewing).

* * * * *

Her relatives were the first ones to settle in this area of Bourbon County in 1869. She had been a slave, and a full-blooded Cherokee Indian helped her escape. As a slave, Hanna had been beaten and had fish hooks placed in her lips. The Cherokee Indian and she had twenty children. One day, her husband returned from the woods hunting and was met by border ruffians who wanted to run them off the land. Linno Sweets (the husband) was knocked off of his horse and beaten to death. One offspring, Glesser Sweets, had his second boy die of frostbite because the house was so cold. Glesser's wife, Kathy, was out walking her young son when two white men stopped her, raped her and took her son with them. Glesser trailed them only to find the body of his dead son in the woods. Later, the wife had one of those men's child (a girl) (Machelle Young).

* * * * *

His dad was known to have the fastest car in town which came in quite handy because he and his brother passed a cop directing traffic. While they were going about 40 to 50 mph, they casually lobbed a full can of beer at the cop, hit him in the chest and nearly knocked him over. The cop jumped in his car and chased them, but the cop could not catch the fast car (Jay Lickteig).

* * * * *

Her mother was named when her grandfather was in the Air Force. All the men in his squadron put various names in a hat, and that is how the mother was named (Darby Willingham).

* * * * *

Her great-great-grandmother was one of those surviving the Trail of Tears in 1838. Fifteen thousand were forced to walk approximately those one thousand miles, and her great-great-grandmother was only twelve years old. Each Indian had a personal roll number that entitled the member to allotments of land. The great-great-grandmother's number was 6501 (Staci Kmiec).

* * * * *

In their family, the name Albert was unlucky because they had five males named Albert and all died prematurely: one of a suicide, one in a car accident, one of a heart attack, one of typhoid at age eight, and one in infancy, cause unknown (Rose Stoughton).

* * * * *

His great-grandma always fished in dresses. One day they had fished for about five to six hours, and when they got home, great-grandma went to the restroom and then began yelling, "Oh, Lola, (her daughter), Oh, Lola, come here." After a few minutes, Grandma came out laughing and crying. We asked what happened? She said that great-grandma had sunburned her crotch (Lee Burns).

* * * * *

Another time when they were fishing, the cork and all came flying at her when she jerked the pole to set the hook. The cork hit her head and split it wide open. Mom was trying to clean up the blood, and all Great-grandma said was, "Leave me alone, Dixie; I am fishing" (Lee Burns).

* * * * *

The relatives of James P. Allen helped establish Allen, New Mexico, when James made application in approximately 1907 to establish a post office in the back of his store (Jack Lockwood).

* * * * *

Her great-grandfather's father, Al Hess, had Hesston, Kansas, named after him, and he donated all of his land for the Hesston College to be built on (Melissa Bailey).

* * * * *

Her cousin, Brian, is a Wicca. This means he is a white witch (Julie May).

* * * * *

His great-grandparents, James and Laura Ross, married in 1879 in West Virginia and then headed across the Allegheny Mountains for 175 miles until they reached a valley twenty miles north of Charleston, West Virginia. They settled there and raised thirteen children. Since James Ross was instrumental in establishing a post office, they were asked to choose a name for the town. They thought for about a week, and finally one morning at about 6 a.m. they heard the pet rooster, "Coco," clucking, so they named the town Coco, and it still exists today (Brian Love).

* * * * *

Her great-great-great-grandfather became general manager of *The Star*. He married a woman who was the madam of a bordello. Once, a man pulled a gun on the relative, and she stepped in and took the bullet. She survived, and they became extremely wealthy people (Jennifer Seested).

* * * * *

A great-great-grandpa, Ervin Andrew Gillmore, was taught to read and write by George Washington Carver. Another relative of the Gillmore family actually owned Carter and his mother (Shanda Jefferis).

* * * * *

A relative, Jacob Carl, born 1855, died 1923, inherited a castle in Scotland, but he never claimed it because of back taxes and the fact that he would have to live in it. His relatives, the Barnards, were the first to have an indoor restroom in the country. Frances Barnard was the governor of Boston until he was forced to go back to England because he was negotiating with the Colonists. A law in Boston said that one side of Boston was not to visit or stay with the other side (Jeff Morris).

* * * * *

Her aunts recall how their grandfather would go out to the bars each night without his wife. The grandmother had her girls urinate into his bottle of hair dye. He never found out, but the grandmother felt that she had had her revenge. He also was capable of throwing the table across the room if the eggs were not cooked right (Barbara Pollom).

* * * * *

A relative came over from Sweden whose name was Johnson. Since many slave owners named their slaves Johnson, this relative wanted to change his name because he sought a better life and the American dream. When he went to the courthouse to change his name, the clerk was impatient and rude and could not understand what he was saying. She looked up and saw his green tie and gave him the last name of "Tiegreen" (Josh Tiegreen).

* * * * *

Sam Wynn of Afton, Oklahoma, was the town marshal and an anti-KKK activist. He was ambushed by the clan on his way to town. They wrestled him to the ground, cut him open and left his entrails on the ground. Later, a man came along and stuffed the marshal's entrails back in and took him to the town doctor who sewed up the stomach, and the marshal lived. Several years later, though, the marshal was found dead, presumably by the clan. He was buried by unknown men in an unknown place so as to protect his wife (Jeremy Wynn).

* * * * *

A relative, William Hardin Alumbaugh, born October 29, 1916, killed himself by ingesting poison. His wife, Evalina, was in a sanitarium suffering from TB, and he had fallen in love with another woman. Rather than betray either woman, he chose to kill himself. Evalina later died in 1942 from TB (Whitney Alumbaugh).

* * * * *

Victor Peterson was chosen, along with ten others, to run an exhibition one-mile race with Glen Cunningham in Salina, Kansas, about 1931. Victor said, "I had to put nails in my shoes in order to have spikes." Glenn had the official spikes for runners. After four laps, Glenn left them all behind. "All I can remember from that race was seeing the heels of him" (Whitney Alumbaugh).

* * * * *

When the Homestead Act was passed in 1862, Frederick Karleskint applied for 160 acres for ten dollars — provided he cleared the land and planted on it. After leaving New York and on to St. Louis, he journeyed westward, but his wife died on the journey. Since there was no Catholic cemetery in Fort Scott, she was buried in St. Paul, Kansas. Seven years later, Frederick donated land for the St. Mary's Catholic Cemetery in Fort Scott and also donated another plot of land for a school to be built. It was known as the Karleskint School many years before it was renamed. Presently, that small frame building still stands west of Fort Scott on the

Humboldt Road where it is used as a private residence (Karleskint).

* * * * *

Her great-grandmother, Mora Jackman, would take food to the outlaws, the James and Younger gang, in caves in Warsaw, Missouri, in a small town called Cross Timbers. A great-uncle Felix would often see balls of fire rise from the ground and appear to be chasing them. Also Mora and her husband remember a gate opening and closing by itself, so they believed it was ghosts (Amanda Pope).

* * * * *

Her grandmother, Mobeth Terrill (also called Madia), had invited relatives for dinner. Grandpa began complaining about the meatloaf and said it was not fit for the dogs. She dumped his meatloaf over his head, whistled for the dozen hound dogs she had collected over the year, and the dogs proceeded to prove it was, indeed, fit for the dogs!! At thirteen, Madia married Voile Edward Eskew. He was an alcoholic and mean, so one night she sewed him into his bedsheet, beat him with a beer bottle, and walked away with nothing but her two children and her mother. She kept walking until she reached Bell Town in Fort Scott and stayed there the remainder of her life (Jeanne Brodnax Fornfiest).

* * * * *

Cody Aikens explained how his Pottawatomi culture used peyote. "We sit in a tepee and pray all night" (this calls up the spirits). Also, the old mishos (grandfathers) sing Peyote songs. My grandma Dorothy always said, "If you end up abusing it, they always say it can come back on you ten times." For example, a relative, John Pah-Mah-Me, used it to pray that he could run like a deer so that he could catch up to one, and he did. He prayed for fish one day and walked to the pond to see ten fish there. After a couple of years, he married and wanted children, but the babies kept dying when reaching about a month old. He went to his misho and he said, "The Great Spirit will always take the most important thing from you and the most sentimental." John quit practicing the peyote for selfish purposes and finally had children (Cody Aikens).

* * * * *

Each new baby is given an Indian color: blue or red. The first-born is blue because they have a blue lower back down to the butt. Every full-blooded Pottawatomi baby that is born first has a baby blue butt. It goes away in time, though (Cody Aikens).

* * * * *

Louis Pommier, born March 19, 1919, said, "If the home that you build for your family is finished, then your life's work is done and you will soon die." As a result, the relative left a two-foot section of the baseboard off in the basement of his house, and the custom was passed on to each of his children (Chris Pommier).

* * * * *

George Springer was born on November 10, 1844, and died December 5, 1876, after an incident where he was fishing in a rowboat when a gust of wind blew a snake out of a nearby tree. It landed directly in George's lap and bit him. He wouldn't go to the doctor, and two weeks later he died. George was the first Springer buried in Mount Vernon Cemetery, northeast of Sedan, Kansas (Sarah Springer).

* * * * *

Another George Springer was born on May 4, 1859, but he died as an infant. While he was sleeping in a rocking chair, he was accidentally sat on by the hired man, and the infant died as a result (Sarah Springer).

* * * * *

A friend of William and Zula Springer stopped at the Springers' home in Yampa, Colorado, in June of 1900. A woman named Carrie Nation was on her way to raid Kiowa Saloons. Zula and her daughters helped Carrie wrap bricks for her raid. Before she left,

Carrie borrowed a bonnet and a hatchet from Zula. She used both items during her raid (Sara Springer).

* * * * *

Her grandmother travels to schools in Linn County to demonstrate how to make lye soap so that children do not forget the ways of the past. Her family also used the soap for poison ivy (Stacy Earnest).

* * * * *

His great-grandpa, Bert, played second base for the old Kansas City Blues baseball team. After a severe broken leg, Bert struggled for jobs in Kansas City. He drove an ice truck and delivered to some of Kansas City's most wealthy and notorious. One was Tom Pendergast. Later, Bert volunteered to be the chauffeur for Pendergast (Brian Boyd).

* * * * *

John Roger Pullin was born on November 14, 1873, in Holt, Missouri, and he married a Martha Ann Franklin who was born on October 5,1879, in Fentress, Tennessee. She was of Osage ancestry. Each owned his/her own chickens, one white and one brown, so as to distinguish between the eggs (because each also earned his/her money. Martha used to steal one of John's egg crates and put it at the bottom of hers each time they went to market. She always had $300 to $400 hidden inside her petticoat (Michael Pullin).

* * * * *

Michael Pullin's father is Dean Pullin. Dean's doctor was drunk when he delivered Dean and put on the wrong date of birth, misspelled his name, and added the wrong sex!! (Michael Pullin).

* * * * *

In land called Warner Bottoms near Walker, Missouri, Noble Elroy Warner told about the early purchase of this land: It was full of snakes. The fields were just snake holes. We told our dad about the snakes, and he said we were lying. One day, he drove his tractor through the fields and looked down at the wheel of the tractor. There were many snakes wrapped around the wheel. He told us not to go out there anymore, but we didn't listen to him. Then again, we never got bit either (Andy Warner).

* * * * *

In this same house, they could sometimes at night hear chains rattling, and it sounded like someone was walking through the house. It sounded almost like a ghost, or so they thought. Since they thought that the ghost possibly came from the cemetery next to the house, no one was ever allowed to go into the cemetery. The stones in the cemetery were marked as Slave 1, Slave 2, etc. (Andy Warner).

* * * * *

Her great-grandma, Roxie Riley, was called "Old Hen" by great-granddad Riley. It made her very mad. Once he went to a bar and had a little too much to drink. When he came home, he called Grandma the "Old Hen," and she busted him in the face with her fist (Heather Hartzfeld).

* * * * *

A relative was raised by another family after both the father and mother died around 1860. This family was very strict. They told the child, Mary Birnah Hall, to sweep the floor, but she didn't do a good enough job, and the mother said, "If you had done a good job, you would have found the dime under the leg of the stove" (Valarie Pape).

* * * * *

Valarie Pape's great-grandmother still holds a pocketbook of George Washington's. The story goes: One day, George Washington was angry and threw his wallet in the trash can. The wallet still had money in it. Tobias Lear, Washington's secretary, took the pocketbook out of the trash and kept it. When he died, Alfred received the wallet from the estate of Tobias Lear. Then, Alfred's brother gave it to him. From then on, it was to be passed to the oldest daughter of each generation. Barbara Farwell, a relative, says it is in a museum in Pennsylvania (Valarie Pape).

* * * * *

April Piatt is pursuing a story she discovered in her genealogy research about a great-uncle, Felix Crawford, who was killed by her great-great-grandmother's first husband, James Long. From a story in *The Enterprise* in Warsaw, Missouri, the shooting occurred as such:

"On Saturday evening, October 20, 1906, a shooting occurred in Alexander township that resulted in the deaths of Felix Crawford and Mrs. Theodosha M. Winemiller. All those involved said the man with the gun was James Long, a son-in-law of Mr. Crawford.

"The deaths occurred at the widow Winemiller's house, a desolate-looking place five miles west of Warsaw, near the junction of the Pomme de Terre and Osage rivers.

"James Long was living with his father-in-law and had left home early Saturday morning and came to Warsaw with some fish, which he sold. While here, he went to the store of Gallaher & Calbert and bought a No. 10-gage double-barrel shotgun, agreeing to pay a dollar a week until the gun was paid for.

"He was drinking and left late Sunday afternoon, in company with Jay McDowell, whom he left at the Joe Crawford Farm on the Fairfield Warsaw road about 7 o'clock. It is reported he did not go home but went straight to the Widow Winemiller's place and began shooting at the house. He shot several times at the front, then walked around to the back and shot out the window, some of the shot coming through a crack in the wall and wounding George Winemiller, age 9, in the left hand.

"Felix Crawford, who lived a short distance from the Winemiller home, heard the shots and started for the home. When he got within 100 feet of the house, he was ordered to halt by Long, who asked who he was and when he answered 'Felix Crawford,' Long shot him, about forty shots hitting him in the side.

"Mrs. Winemiller and her two daughters, Ida and Cinderella, then ran out where the men were, and Long shot Widow Winemiller in the left side at close range, the fire from the gun setting fire to her clothing. She never regained consciousness and died in about 15 minutes.

"In the meantime, the two young girls had carried their mother into the house and did everything in their power to save her life, but she died in a few minutes. Long forced them to give him matches and he lit a lantern and found part of his gun, which had been lost in the scuffle with Crawford. He told them not to go after help, that he would go and he disappeared.

"The young ladies then turned their attention to Crawford, who told them to go to Joe Crawford's about three-quarters of a mile away and telephone for a doctor. This Cinderella did. Each of the girls made several trips to the home of neighbors and showed remarkable bravery and courage. They did everything possible for the dying man until Dr. Dillon and Wm. Salley of Fairfield arrived and took Crawford's dying statement.

"Sheriff Hart was notified of the crime by telephone and, in company of Deputy Bagwell and several others, arrived on the scene between eleven and midnight. Few of the party were armed, and it was not thought advisable to make a search for Long until morning. Telephone messages were sent to Warsaw for shotguns, and all nearby towns were notified to be on the lookout for him. A crowd arrived from Warsaw before daylight, with shotguns, and a diligent search was made of the surrounding country, but the only trace of Long was where he had crossed the river in his boat and turned it loose."

April Piatt reported of an abandoned cemetery outside of Warsaw, Missouri, with about twenty graves, and she wants to further investigate the history of those connected with this time period (April Piatt).

* * * * *

Alan Shepherd's grandmother, Bonita Shumate, met her husband (Alan's grandfather-to-be, Irvin Day) when he came up and said to Bonita, "Hold my raffle ticket. The prize is a turkey and you are going to cook it for me. In fact, you are going to cook all my meals from now on" (Alan Shepherd).

* * * * *

William Westhues came from Germany in 1848. He had five boys and one girl when the couple took their family to Glasgow, Missouri. Realizing that all of his children could not take over the farm, he set up a plan: if they wanted an education, he would pay for it; if they stayed to farm until age twenty-one, they received a horse and buggy and $250 a year for savings, plus spending money; if they stayed until twenty-eight, they got $1,000, three horses, a plow, wagon, harrow, two cows and two sows (Jimmy Stuart).

*****

Her great-great-grandfather, William Henry, left home because he felt responsible for his brother's death, so he hit the road. In his travels, he befriended Buffalo Bill Cody. Cody picked him up on the trail and told him he would have to work in his show to pay his own way. Buffalo Bill even took care of him while he had typhoid fever (Jessica Roberts).

*****

Her grandma recalls lots of gypsies around Hermitage, Missouri. When the grandmother was a baby, the gypsies knocked on the door to ask for food. While the mother went down into the cellar to get them food, they stole the baby. The mother blew on the conch shell twice, and her husband, who was out in the fields working, jumped on his horse and chased them. Luckily, he got his daughter back (Kari Stewart).

*****

His grandpa, James Stewart, lived in a part of Indiana known as Stone County because of its many stone mills. His father was a stone tooler and was carving a stone for the Eisenhower Museum. President Eisenhower put the piece of stone on the museum himself. The grandfather also tooled a piece of stone depicting a Kansas pioneer couple on the Docking building in Topeka, Kansas (Justin Talley).

* * * * *

The Newkirk family named their son Jedidiah James Newkirk and called him "J.J.," but he never looked like a "J.J.," so they began calling him Jed. When his sister, Jalaynna, was born, she was put in a twin bed at twelve months because every morning the parents would find Jed in her crib sleeping soundly with Jalaynna in his arms. The parents were afraid the crib would collapse and hurt them. Jed also attended the United Methodist preschool at the age of four but was expelled from preschool for hitting a child with a Tonka truck. The child he hit had taken the truck from one of Jed's friends. Jed's response was, "I was just trying to help" (Jed Newkirk).

* * * * *

In April of 1835 in Wales, his great-grandmother's father, John Tomlinson, was born. He became a caleminor, which in those days was one who painted the walls in a house. The paint would wash off, so they would wash and paint them again. When he wanted to make his parents mad, he used to lick his finger and rub the paint off (Tyson Rae).

* * * * *

When Matt Johnson's father got into trouble as a young boy, his dad (Matt's grandfather and also a high school teacher) would punish students by having them copy out of dictionaries or encyclopedias in the study hall. "I think I copied the whole book," said Matt's father (Matt Johnson).

* * * * *

Benjamin Leroy Jackson was born on July 4, 1888, in Indiana; he married Alice Mae Shannon in Marshalltown, Iowa, and they had eight children. During the depression, Alice died of diphtheria, so the family was quarantined. The doctor made house calls, and one of the twin boys, Frank, was ill so often that they decided to remove his tonsils, but the family had no means of payment. Since the house did not have electricity, an extension cord was run from the neighbor's house to supply a source of electricity for the doctor to have light. Frank was placed on the kitchen table and held down by his father and two older children while the doctor did the surgery. No anesthetic was used (Justin Jackson).

* * * * *

"Noodling" was when the children would stand very still in the river and would reach into caves or mud holes in the riverbank and swiftly catch the fish inside or catch those swimming by in the river current (Kristin Boyd).

* * * * *

Elvy and Augustas (Gussy) Baker Shackelford were farming together near Statesbury, Missouri, when the rain started to pour. The brothers were walking side by side in the field when Elvy remembered he forgot his jacket. He was blown up into the air and knocked unconscious. Elvy woke up to learn that his brother, Gussy, had been struck in the head and killed by lightning less than fifty feet from Elvy's jacket (Kristin Boyd).

* * * * *

His mother was born on September 4, 1948. She was born with eleven fingers and was one of eleven children. She also had a daughter who had twelve fingers (Aaron Bell).

* * * * *

In 1899, George Washington Mizer tried to save his farm in Arcadia, Nebraska, from a fire. After a hopeless battle, he attempted to cross a creek to save his life. However, as he descended the bank, the flames swept upon him, and when finally picked up his clothes were burned off and his flesh fairly cooked (Jennifer Milano).

* * * * *

His grandfather was the first person to own a tractor in Bourbon County (Jeremiah Hill).

* * * * *

Maxine Simon, Katy Mena's great-grandmother, washes her cranberries in the washing machine to make sure they are clean before making cranberry bread, and she also paints her house every summer with whatever color is on sale (Katy Mena).

* * * * *

Mary Wood recalls a time that she and her brothers witnessed a baptism. After it was over, the boys came home and dug a hole in the yard and filled it with water. Then they took her dolls and said, "In the name of the Father and the Son, and in the hole you go." The boys dunked several of the dolls before Wilma Underwood, their mother, could stop them (Tracy Homan).

* * * * *

Amanda Cowen said that her great-great-grandfather told his two girls never to go near the street because he was afraid of the two girls being hurt or kidnapped. One day, they waited for him to come from work at the street corner. He spanked the older girl, Agnes. The mother decided to spare the younger daughter, Peggy, from his punishment, so she picked Peggy up and hid her under a bed. He swung underneath the bed to swat Peggy, but accidentally missed her and hit the mother. The mother divorced him for battery (Amanda Cowen). Also, when Agnes Boyle (Amanda's great-grandmother) died of a brain seizure, no embalming was done since the family could not afford it. Agnes' daughter, Margaret, started looking for her mother and found her in the sitting room lying in a bed, dead, foaming at the mouth and starting to decompose. Margaret Boyle was so traumatized by seeing her mother that she did not speak for one year (Amanda Cowen).

* * * * *

Lerin Henry's grandmother remembers when her own mother died there was an upside-down rainbow. Everyone believed that the rainbow showed them that Great-grandmother Harris had made it to heaven and was happy. Another Hoskin family belief is in angels. When that Harris great-grandmother passed away, Grandmother Hoskin and Arley were sitting in their house talking about Great-grandmother Harris' death. They looked at a jewelry box that she had given Arley, and all of a sudden it opened and started playing music. To this day, everyone believes that Great-grandmother Harris is watching over us and lets us know it every once in awhile (Lerin Henry).

* * * * *

Sydney Hotsenpiller was a teacher in Smithton, Missouri. He had two brothers in the school who bragged about making teachers eventually quit, but Sydney explained he was there to stay. When one of the brothers gave him trouble for the first time, he took a hitching rein and tied the brother to a fence. Sydney told him that when he could behave, wave and someone would come out and untie him. It then started to rain, and the brother continued to sit out there. Not until two hours later (and a thorough drenching) did the boy finally wave. "This ornery behavior by great-grandmother could not happen in today's world of education, but I think in some cases it would definitely get the point across!" (Christy Hotsenpiller).

* * * * *

Ross Riley told of experiences in World War II aboard the *USS California:* All sailors who had never crossed the equator were dressed as babies. They wore cloth dishtowels as diapers and had to suck their thumbs and act like a baby and then were expected to crawl on their bellies in garbage such as coffee ground, chicken entrails and rotten food. If they did not obey, they were beaten with clubs that had been soaked in salt water to harden the boards. As soon as they passed, or survived the ceremony, they were known as the "polliwogs," and they also received identification cards stating their achievement and accomplishment (Troy Schaub).

* * * * *

When Lucas Coppinger's grandfather and his grandfather's brother, George, were young, their dad told them that they could have all of the baby pigs that were born bobtailed (knowing all the time that pigs aren't bobtailed). The boys went outside and found the sow having babies, and they actually bit the pigs' tails off (Lucas Coppinger).

* * * * *

When Joe Robinson's great-great-grandfather, Henry Luebbe, came from Germany and settled in the Wells Creek near Belvue, Kansas, he married Etta Pagelir, and their first child, Esther, was born with what they called a "veil" over her face. This was a thin skin covering the face, and it doesn't happen very often. Therefore, she was believed to be able to tell the future when she grew up. In fact, she told fortunes and was said to be quite accurate (Joe Robinson).

* * * * *

Yale, Kansas, was located where Chicken

Annie's and Chicken Mary's are now (Jessica Roberts).

* * * * *

The first white settlers in Vernon County, Missouri, were the Summers brothers in the early 1800s. One of these brothers was named Jesse J. Summers who was born in North Carolina in 1794. He settled in the area that is now known as Metz, Missouri. Jesse married a woman named Charlotte McDermid who was born in Kentucky in 1800. Together they had one son whom they also named Jesse. He later went on to marry a woman from the Fort Scott area named Surilla Ann Johnson. They had a son named Rolla Lee Summers and another son named Will. Both brothers ran a still together in Cedar County in the '20s, and once, when both were drunk, they argued over some profits they had made. Zora arrived just in time to see Will shoot Rolla in the head. Will then drew on Zora, but before he had a chance to shoot, the dog took him, and Zora ran to the neighbors' home for help. Will got loose from the dog and shot it; then he made his escape. After a long manhunt, he was finally caught around Clinton, Missouri. Will's mother's family had money, and after only three years they petitioned him out of jail. He then went to his own home where his wife, three daughters, son-in-law and grandchild lived. He shot the house up by wounding his wife and son-in-law. After a long siege with the police, he was taken to the Nevada State Hospital where he remained until he died He is buried in an unmarked grave at the State Hospital Cemetery (Michael Pullin).

* * * * *

My grandma's side of the family was very poor. There were four kids in her family, and they didn't have enough money for the necessities of life. My grandma's dad would hunt rabbits for them to eat. He would bring them home and hang them off the front porch. All of the kids would get really embarrassed. At meals, they would have three pieces of bread for all six of them. Her mom would get one, her dad another one, and the four kids would have to split the third piece of bread. Since they didn't have enough money for food, doctors weren't on the priority list either. Once my great-grandpa had a corn on his toe. It started to get cold and pain badly, so he went outside and put his foot up on a log, took an ax and chopped it right off. When my grandma needed a haircut, she asked her dad for one. He got mad and shaved off her long blond hair down to an inch of length. When it grew back, it was bright red (Brandie Albaugh).

* * * * *

Even though Grandfather Endicott could not read or write, he obtained a driver's license. However, he never drove alone as he needed someone to read the road signs for him. Also, he belied in voting in each and every election. Each election, Grandmother would go into the booth and read the ballot for him. They did this until 1960 when Grandfather was informed that both a Democrat and a Republican would have to witness the marking of the ballot. This was to ensure that Grandmother marked it according to Grandfather's wishes. Grandfather was outraged and vowed never to vote again (Karen Rains).

* * * * *

Grandfather and Grandmother Endicott were members of the Cherry Grove Baptist Church. For several years they attended services on a regular basis. However, on one Sunday the minister informed Grandfather that he had to tithe 10 percent of his earnings. Grandfather felt that he couldn't afford to give that amount, and he instructed Grandmother to collect the children because they were going home. He always said that his family came first. Grandfather never again attended church services. Grandfather, though, was known as a hard worker and an honest man. Neighbors often came to him for advice, and he often purchased a cemetery plot if a family could not afford one (Karen Rains).

* * * * *

Sayings

I will beat your butt till it barks like a fox.

A strong family is a family who can depend on one another even when the sun ain't shining.

A relative was going to marry a divorced woman, but his grandmother told him to tell his family: 'Soup is always better warmed over."

If I can find a dollar bill rolling up hill, I'll give it to you.

To be called a snake eater means you don't like them.

If it doesn't work in, it will work out.

He has too many witnesses to remain in office for long.

If it is too thick to walk in, it is too wet to plow.

If you do not finish a project, you go to "half-done land."

A hard head will make a soft ass.

There is much good in the worst of us, and so much bad in the best of us, that it hardly behooves any of us to talk about the rest of us.

When you feel that you are better than anyone else, put your finger in a glass of water. When you remove your finger, the hole you leave behind is how much more important you are than anyone else.

Anyone lose a dollar? I found a penny of it.

You are as dumb as a broom straw.

You are as handy as a pocket on a shirt.

Put a little pot in the big one, and we'll be in to eat.

About marriage: "If you go fishing in a sewer, you will catch a rat."

Everybody in this world is as good as I am, but damn few better.

We had running water — you ran outdoors and got it.

If it was worth washing, it was worth ironing.

Idle hands make for evil minds.

It is what you learn after you know it that counts.

Can't is a bastard too lazy to work.

The devil owed me a debt and paid me off in sons-in-law.

If I die before I wake, wash my dirty feet.

For someone inept: "You couldn't drive a cat into a smokehouse."

Don't take more than you can eat, and eat what you take.

You don't have a pot to piss in nor a window to throw it out of.

It is so small that you couldn't have a cat in

here without getting fur in your mouth.

When children nag for things: "You can when pigs grow wings."

Never ask any more of your parents as long as they provide a roof over your head.

We were so poor that they cut holes in the boys' pockets so that they could have something to play with.

When Ma said, "Shit," you could smell it.

Don't leave your nest so shitty you can't crawl back into it.

Come on in if your nose is clean.

You can fly high and shit in the air, but you have to come down for water.

Looks like a duck peeking for thunder.

I would rather help the needy than the greedy.

You will never own anything unless you work for it and buy it yourself.

You may not be sure where you are going, but never forget where you come from.

To teach swimming (the old-fashioned way), "Throw them in and pluck them out."

If I live one hundred years, I could not make you be good, if you did not want to. If I die tomorrow, no one else can make you be bad, if you don't want to.

It is colder than a well-digger's butt.

The world has come to a rush.

You can take one stick and break it. You can take two sticks and bend them. You can take three sticks and twist them. If you take more, you will have a hard time to break, bend or twist. Stick together.

People in Hell want ice water, too.

A liar will steal and a stealer will kill.

It is nice to be important, but is more important to be nice.

Only one life and soon it will pass; only what is done for Christ will last.

That is slick as snot on a doorknob.

If my auntie had balls, she'd be my uncle.

Boy, I wish I had that and he had a feather. Then we'd both be tickled to death.

Ex-lax is the strongest thing there is. It can even knock the shit out of superman.

Superstitions

Don't cut toenails or fingernails on a Sunday as it is bad luck.

If you forget something, sit down and count to ten before returning to the car, or else you will have a wreck.

Hang out the clothes before a rain, and it will be like a fabric softener.

When it rains on Monday, it will rain two more days that week.

If you move to a different house, you have to cut a piece of hair off of the end of the dog's tail and put it on your back step. If you do this, your dog will never leave home.

If it thunders in February, it will frost in May.

Never plow ground in January as it sleeps that month.

A whistling girl and a crowing hen always come to a bad end.

Witch wells with a forked peach tree limb, and they will never go dry.

When it is raining and the sun is shining at the same time, it means that the devil is beating his wife.

When you leave home and forget something and have to go back to get it, always sit back down in the last chair that you were sitting in.

If someone gives you a knife, pay him for it, or it will cut off friendship.

If a black cat crosses your path, mark an X on the windshield and spit out the window.

Keep a glass egg in the nest so chickens will lay more eggs.

Do not touch the tomatoes or green beans, etc., during menstrual periods, or it will cause them to spoil.

During a storm, sit in the middle of a feather bed because lightning won't strike a feather bed.

If a person is cut with a knife or any sharp object, the victim should take the object to the yard and stick it directly into the dirt or bury it, and the bleeding will stop.

How to make babies tall: stretch the baby's back by holding him by the heel and stroking his back while the baby is hanging upside down. Do this every day through the baby's first year.

During the seven days before Christmas, if four out of the seven were full moon, there will be good crops. If the reverse is true, there will be bad crops.

If a broom falls across the doorway, company is coming.

Don't marry on a Friday.

Put kerosene on bedposts for bed bugs.

Friday begun, never done.

Don't go barefoot before May 1st and not after September 1st.

All farmers who had to move tried to do so on March 1st. This was true for people around St. Paul, Kansas (Jean Stocks' grandfather, Charles Lero).

The first-born son is named Michael Silvestro or Silvestro Michael, and every generation it is reversed. That trend continued until 1951 when the more Americanized name of Silvester became only the middle name (Matt Altieri).

A snake always strikes the second one if you and others are walking through a pasture.

Don't wear blue on a Monday.

If a turtle crosses the road, it will rain.

Spit on the worms for good luck while fishing.

The longer the umbilical cord stays attached, the better chance for a child's health.

Do not sweep the floor at night.

Never do the washing on a Good Friday, or it will bring death.

Do not walk over a wagon tail, or someone will get sick or die.

If you dream of muddy water, it means death.

Always milk a cow on the right side.

Throw a hat on the bed, and you will have bad luck.

You cannot put two lighted lanterns on a table at once.

It is bad luck to close a pocket knife after someone else opened it.

Sprinkling red pepper over the door will prevent enemies from entering.

Do not drink milk and eat fish in the same meal, or you will die.

If at night you see a glow or light, it means death.

If there is sunshine coming through apple trees on Christmas Day, there will be good crops the next year.

The earlier that a hen starts eating, the better eggs they produce.

Many Indian clans are named after animals.

The clans believe you cannot eat or kill that specific animal. The only thing you can do is help it. If you do not, you will get sick and get sores.

Beaus won't come where cobwebs grow.

If a child has asthma, take him outside and make a mark on a tree. When he outgrows this mark, he won't have asthma.

Remedies

To cure a cranky baby who is cutting teeth, put an egg in a ziplock bag, place it in a butter bowl in the same dresser drawer with the baby's clothes, and you won't have a problem with the baby's cutting teeth.

If a child is pigeon-toed, put his shoes on the wrong feet to correct it.

To kill a cricket in the house is bad luck, and if a cricket sings to you in the house, you are going to get some money.

Never sweep under a single person's feet because he will never get married.

Use cigar ashes and lard to get rid of ringworms.

Wear black silk thread around the throat for protection against upper respiratory infection.

If you give a painted object to a girl, then you must collect a penny from that person.

Abby Lawrence's family used Watkins Liniment as a cure-all for everything: bites, cuts, bruises, splinters. The recipe was to use two tablespoons in orange juice. When Abby's father was nineteen, he crushed his leg in a motorcycle wreck. Gangrene set in, and after spending six months in the hospital in traction, his mom used liniment religiously on his foot, and it drew all of the gangrene out.

Use two teaspoons of honey for a stomach ache.

Use scorched flour for baby rash.

Put egg white on burns so that it will not scar.

The best time to wean babies is by the sign of the knees.

Spread cow manure on the skin, and it takes the tan away.

For headache, soak your feet in hot water and go to bed.

Getting a haircut is a remedy for a headache.

Carbolic salve is good for ailments.

For a cut: wash with water, pour turpentine onto the cut, wrap it with a white cloth, and tie a bandage on with a piece of cloth.

Put turpentine and lard on a sore throat and wrap with a cloth.

If you put a wedding ring on a pinkeye, the pinkeye will go away.

Put one-half of a lemon in a small glass of hot water and drink before breakfast to cure a headache.

Put onions and sugar in an oven and bake. Drink the juice for a cold.

To cure colic, put a cotton ball soaked in whiskey on the baby's navel.

Recipe for liniment: bottle of alcohol, twelve crushed aspirins, and a bottle of wintergreen oil.

For warts: rub the wart with a kernel of corn and put the kernel under a rock.

For colic or fussiness: take a skillet, turn it upside down, and put it in the oven.

For a boil: cut the bark of an Elm tree and make a paste.

A musterdine leaf in vinegar will relieve a headache.

If you rub a penny on a wart and then bury the penny, the wart will go away.

Use cow manure to decrease swelling of the legs.

Put perishables in a well, and they will remain at 40 degrees all year.

Dig a hole in a hill and put in the vegetables; then cover with straw.

To get rid of warts: find an old penny with green on it; rub it on the wart, and then throw the penny behind you. Walk away and don't go back for it. Whoever picks up the penny will get the wart.

Use castor oil on warts.

Use one teaspoon of Certo to a glass of water for arthritis.

A green walnut shell will clear up poison ivy. The darker color it turns your skin, the better it works.

Put sugar on a cut to stop the bleeding. It absorbs and makes the blood clot faster.

If you take a bandana full of roly-poly bugs, roll them up and wrap them around your neck; they will clear up any chest congestion.

Put a poultice of fried onions on the chest for relief of cold.

Use onions, flax seed, and lard as a mixture for a poultice.

Camille tea cures everything.

For a cold, use lemon tea, cinnamon, honey, and Jack Daniels.

Take soot and boil it; after it cools, add sugar and feed to infants to stop their coughing.

A baked potato will help cure a stomach ache.

Use cod liver oil, honey, and aspirin for colds.

Put peppermint tobacco on bee stings.

For burns, use bread soaked in milk to apply to the burn.

Mashed walnuts will cure an earache.

Blow baking soda on the tonsils with a straw for the sore throat.

Breathe into your hand to get rid of the hiccups.

Soak your feet in your own urine to get rid of athletes' feet.

For a nosebleed, read something from John in the Bible.

Apply kerosene to a snake bite. If the kerosene turns green, there is still poison. Continue until kerosene is clear.

Use milk and bread poultice for a rusty nail. Apply to a rag and keep wrapped for three days.

Put spider webs on cuts from shaving.

Use garlic for high blood pressure.

For warts: take a washrag from Grandma

or Great-grandmother, and bury it, and the warts will go away.

For colds: 1 drop of sugar, 1 drop of turpentine; roll this in onion skin; take goosegrease and rub all of this on the neck for colds.

If you use soot on a cut, you will never have a scar.

For diarrhea: raw eggs, vinegar, and pepper.

Mistakes

In the overall picture of assessment of a college paper, a grader tends to focus on the most major correctional needs within the least amount of time. In other words, a teacher tries for positive comments while at the same time trying to assess the submissions in a thorough manner that enables students to receive speedy feedback on suggestions before the due date of the next assigned paper. Therefore one's objective was not to concentrate on the "goofs" but to make the objective a learning, positive experience. Time did not allow to do both grading and recording, but, nevertheless, I could not pass up the temptation to record a few of the more "classic errors." The following errors help maintain one's sense of humor along with the job at hand (I would shudder to think of my own errors had the students collectively amassed their own lists):

* * * * *

"I know I wouldn't want to live just on my organs alone."

* * * * *

After giving a test over *Catcher In The Rye,* I remarked in a chastising tone that 99 percent of the class flunked the test. A student said, "I'm going to tell Mom I am in the 99 percentile of my class!"

* * * * *

A student wrote: "I want to be a teacher to mold and fertilize the mind."

* * * * *

"We should be in the Middle East. There are insent people and moral values at steak."

* * * * *

"My stranger I call alcoholism. It stripped all my valves away."

* * * * *

"After all, it's not every day that you may have a little being growing inside of you."

* * * * *

"I have a friend who just commented suicide."

* * * * *

"I sure hope my feelings get consecutive."

* * * * *

"He approached me and we became deep in conservation."

* * * * *

"Many things can happen in a relationship, and being defied of friendship is one of them."

* * * * *

"Lois died of step throat."

* * * * *

"She was a very witted lady who always liked a good laugh."

* * * * *

"Her brother would get her down on the floor and tickle her until she would start to laugh and then spit down her thought."

* * * * *

"Virginia, the oldest girl, was the attitude of the family."

* * * * *

"Sometimes when all the ships are down and you have no one else to turn to."

* * * * *

"Brides'maid (possessive)."

* * * * *

"But there are goods with the bads.'

* * * * *

"Cindy's life started to fall peas by peas."

* * * * *

"The only kind of income she gets is well fare and her oldest daters social security."

* * * * *

"Although numerous other impacts on my youth are memorable, divorce still stinks in my quest for togetherness."

* * * * *

"My father bolted around the corner, burning up, in his car."

* * * * *

"That evening, my parents took my brother and I out to dinner, rare at a nice restaurant."

* * * * *

From an Assignment over *Death of a Salesman*

"Let's ease drop on Willy's final conversation with his boss."

"When he takes these bribes, he is just setting himself on a pedalstool."

"Miller presents Happy as a merry-go-lucky-kind of guy."

* * * * *

I assigned a report on existentialism to a student and said to find out what it means and give a five to seven-minute report. He said, "I can't even spell it, let alone find out what it means."

When I had a movie that had

commercials, I asked a boy on the front row if he would please use the remote control to by-pass the commercials. He so enjoyed using it, that he asked to do it the next class period.

A fellow teacher one year said he saw this written on the men's restroom wall: "Verjins is an indanjered speces."

*   *   *

Notes Left for a Teacher

"Ms Dudley:
  Came by to tell you what an inspiring instructor you are . . . also to say I won't be in 102 tomorrow. I'll try to stop by and get my assignments for tomorrow.
Your ardent admirer"

A boy writes from the jail and addresses it to "Mr. Thieking and Mrs. English 101," and then signs it,
"Inconveniently yours"

EDITOR'S NOTE: Addressing the problem of why students do not read, I once, out of frustration and lack of patience, which I am pleased to go on record as not happening that often, asked students on an essay exam to add why they did so poorly with the objective part of *I Heard the Owl Call My Name* which is no more than one hundred and seventy-some pages and is a seventh-grade reading novella. Keep in mind that a book, or novella, is assigned at the beginning of a semester and is the last assignment to accomplish before ending the semester. Also, the assignment is listed on each student's syllabus with the reminder of the due date as often as three to four times throughout the semester. Here were a few of the responses:

"The reason I couldn't do a seventh-grade reading level is because my reading level is fifth grade. As a college student, I'm not prepared to read a novel. When I read a book or novel, I can't tell you anything about what happened in the book as you may already know by the answers to the other questions."

* * * * *

"I didn't have the book ready by that time. I read it that night. Honestly, I thought we were reading it in class. I must have misunderstood, but it was a good book."

* * * * *

"Well, one good reason is that I have no electricity and I overslept. I believe also that my reading level is good. And third I'm always prepared to read a novel, but I got to first find one that keeps my attention."

* * * * *

"I assume that the reason I did so bad would go back to skipping class. I didn't even know we were supposed to be reading the book until the day before the test. If I had been in class I would have known that we were supposed to read the book and that we were having a test. I tried to read the book after I got off of work, but it was hard to get interested in because of the beginning. Even though I did read a lot of it before the test, I read it so fast that I couldn't remember who was who because there were so many names. I love to read, but I just messed myself up by skipping class."

* * * * *

"I don't think I could read a novel for the simple fact that I hate reading."

* * * * *

"The reason I failed was because I did not read the book. I did not realize we had to have it read so quickly, and I had only read the first chapter. I am sorry that I failed, but now I have read the book in the entirety. And that is the honest truth."

* * * * *

"I failed the test last Friday because I did

not know we were having the test and I did not know we needed to have the book read. I do not know whose fault that is, but I will not take all of the blame. Next time please make it easier for all students when these things are going to happen. I have had these misunderstandings with this class a few other times."

* * * * *

"When faced with the everyday challenges of life, I usually win. However, I have failed miserably at college. I really am not focused and ready to settle down. This is my own fault, along with the high school I came from. The teachers never pushed us to what we could have been. I never have felt that I have given my all to school. As a result, when I took a baby step to FSCC, I was not prepared to study for college. I hope that next semester will go much better for myself."